Help!

"Why don't we ask Mrs. Ramirez to set the ballerina painting aside for you until your doll and your CD's sell?" Nancy said to Bess.

Bess sighed. "I already asked her. She said that wouldn't be fair to the family that's selling the painting. I mean, if my stuff doesn't sell and I can't buy the painting, then the family might not get *their* money."

Nancy reached into her pocket. "You have two dollars, and I have one. Even if I gave you this, we'd still need seven more—"

"Nancy! Bess!" George came running up to them. "Did you guys move it?"

"Move what?" Nancy asked her.

"The balleri[...] re-plied breathl[...]

The Nancy Drew Notebooks

Available from MINSTREL Books

THE
NANCY DREW
NOTEBOOKS®

#34

Trash or Treasure?

CAROLYN KEENE
ILLUSTRATED BY JAN NAIMO JONES

A MINSTREL® BOOK

Published by POCKET BOOKS
New York   London   Toronto   Sydney   Singapore

A MINSTREL PAPERBACK *Original*

 A Minstrel Book published by
POCKET BOOKS, a division of Simon & Schuster Inc.
1230 Avenue of the Americas, New York, NY 10020

ISBN: 0-671-03873-7

First Minstrel Books printing February 2000

10 9 8 7 6 5 4 3 2 1

Cover art by Joanie Schwarz

Printed in the U.S.A.

PHX/

1

The Ballerina Painting

This is really cool!" eight-year-old Nancy Drew said. She held up a long, skinny lamp filled with red and orange goo.

"I think it's kind of gross," Nancy's best friend Bess Marvin said, wrinkling her nose. "What *is* that stuff in there?"

George Fayne, Bess's cousin and Nancy's other best friend, laughed. "I don't know, but you'd better not let the customers hear you calling it gross, or no one will buy it," she said.

Nancy, Bess, and George were helping out at a weekend-long garage sale. A bunch of families in Nancy's neighborhood had organized it, and it was being held at the Ramirezes' house. Rebecca Ramirez was a friend of Nancy's, but she was in a different third-grade class at Carl Sandburg Elementary School.

It was an hour before the sale was set to start, and the Ramirezes' garage and driveway were hopping with activity. Neighbors kept coming by with boxes of stuff to sell. Nancy, Bess, and George were taking all the items out of the boxes and arranging them on card tables. Rebecca's brother, Todd, who was twelve years old, was helping a neighbor unload some used furniture from a pickup truck.

"We have to keep track of who's selling what," Mrs. Ramirez told Rebecca. The two of them were sticking price tags on everything.

Mrs. Ramirez pointed to the goo-filled lamp Nancy was holding. "For example, the Hilliards are selling this lava lamp."

"Lava? You mean, like the stuff that

2

comes out of volcanoes?" Bess said, her blue eyes wide.

"It's not *real* lava, Bess," Mrs. Ramirez said with a smile. She glanced down at her clipboard, and then up at Rebecca. "On this list, the Hilliards are number twelve. So you need to write 'number twelve' on the price tag. And as far as the price goes . . . let's see, how about five dollars?"

"Sure," Rebecca said. She uncapped her purple magic marker and picked up a sheet of small white stickers. She wrote: "#12/$5." Then she peeled off the sticker and stuck it to the base of the lamp. "Piece of cake!"

George pulled an old leather baseball glove out of one of the boxes. "I'm selling this. What number am I?"

Rebecca peered at her mother's clipboard. "You're number five, George. How much do you want to sell it for?"

"How about two dollars?" George suggested. Rebecca nodded and wrote "#5/$2" on one of the stickers.

All the girls were selling things they had outgrown. Nancy was selling a parka that was too small. Bess was selling a doll she no longer played with and half a dozen CD's she no longer listened to. Rebecca was selling her Halloween costumes from last year and the year before. And in addition to her baseball glove, George was selling her old toy kitchen, which had been sitting in her family's basement for a long time.

Nancy reached into another box and pulled out a pen that was lying in a dusty candy dish. It wasn't like the ball-point pens she had at home. It was pretty and gold-colored and engraved with the initial *N*.

"N for Nancy!" she said to her friends. "I'm going to buy this later, if I make money from my parka. I can write in my blue notebook with it." Nancy was the best detective at her school, and she liked to solve mysteries. Her dad had given her a special notebook with a shiny blue cover in which to write her clues.

"I've already decided what I'm going to buy," Rebecca said. She picked up a necklace that was lying on the card table and held it up to her neck. It was made of pink glass beads that shone in the light. "Isn't it totally awesome? It's my favorite color!"

"I'm trying to decide between a bunch of comic books and this cool old game called Train Robbery," George said.

Bess frowned and glanced around. "What am *I* going to buy?"

Rebecca pointed to a box of vintage hats. There was a black one with feathers, a red one with satin ribbons, and even one covered with plastic flowers and fruit. "How about one of those hats? They're really cool."

Bess shook her head, which made her blond ponytail bounce back and forth. "I don't know. I'm not in a hat mood today." And then her eyes lit up. "There it is— *that's* what I want to buy!"

She pointed to a painting that was propped against the leg of a gray card table. Painted on canvas, it was a picture of a young ballerina in a white tutu with tiny white flowers on it. She was standing on pointe, with her arms stretched gracefully to one side.

Bess bent down in front of the painting. "Isn't it beautiful?" she said breathlessly. "It would be perfect for my room."

Mrs. Ramirez peeked at her clipboard. "The seller asked that we put ten dollars on that painting." She scribbled "#23/$10" on a sticker and stuck it to the back of the canvas.

"Ten dollars!" Bess groaned. "That's too much money! I bought a new CD at the mall yesterday, and I only have two dollars left from my allowance."

"Maybe you'll have enough money after you sell your old CD's and your doll," Nancy said helpfully.

Bess looked doubtful. "I guess. I just hope no one buys the painting before my stuff sells."

Mrs. Ramirez tapped on her watch. "Speaking of which—the sale starts in half an hour. We'd better get back to work, girls. The customers will be here soon."

The five of them continued to unpack boxes and stick price tags on all the merchandise. It was an unusually warm day for April, and as they worked, Nancy got hot and thirsty—and a little hungry, too. She was glad Mrs. Ramirez had set up a table with juice and blueberry muffins for the volunteers.

At eight-thirty, customers started to show up. Nancy didn't recognize any of them at first. There was a tall, dark-haired man wearing a suit and bow tie. There was a couple with a cute little baby. And there was a short, red-haired woman dressed in a paint-spattered sundress. They were wandering through the yard and the driveway, picking stuff up and inspecting it.

"I guess no one paid attention to the part of the ad that said, 'No Early Birds,'" Mrs. Ramirez said with a sigh.

"Early birds?" George repeated.

"It's a standard rule with garage sales. Sometimes people show up before the sale officially starts to try to buy the good stuff before everyone else. They're called early birds." Mrs. Ramirez shrugged. "I suppose it can't hurt to let these people look around—but no one buys anything before nine o'clock sharp, okay?"

"Okay," Rebecca said, nodding. "Hey, speaking of early birds . . ."

Nancy followed Rebecca's gaze. Brenda Carlton and Alison Wegman were coming up the driveway. Brenda and Alison went to Carl Sandburg Elementary School, too. Brenda had her own newspaper, the *Carlton News*, which her dad helped her do on the computer. Alison was Brenda's best friend.

"Looks like a bunch of junk to me," Brenda said to Alison, glancing around. Then she pointed to Bess's ballerina painting. "Except for that," she added.

"It is kind of cool," Alison agreed.

"It's *super* cool," Brenda said. She

walked up to the painting and picked it up. "Wouldn't it look great in my bedroom?"

Nancy noticed that Bess had stopped unpacking boxes and was listening intently to Brenda and Alison's conversation.

"Sure," Alison said to Brenda. "How much is it?"

Brenda peered at the price tag. "Ten dollars." She put the painting down, reached into her jeans pocket, and fished out a ten-dollar bill. "Hey, that's exactly what I've got. Hmm, maybe I'll buy it."

Bess rushed up to Nancy and grabbed her arm. "Brenda wants my painting," she whispered. "There's no way I'm going to get it now!"

2
Missing!

Rebecca put down her stickers and purple marking pen. Then she strolled over to Brenda and Alison. She, too, had been listening to their conversation about the ballerina painting.

"Brenda, Alison, hi!" Rebecca said with a big smile. "Did you find anything to buy yet?"

"Brenda's maybe going to buy this painting for her room," Alison said. "I haven't found anything yet."

Nancy and Bess moved a little closer so they could hear what the three girls were talking about. Nancy could tell that

Rebecca was up to something, but she wasn't sure what.

Rebecca leaned toward Alison and lowered her voice ever so slightly. Rebecca wanted to be an actress when she grew up, and she was good at being dramatic about things.

"This is just between us, okay?" she said to Alison. "We just got a box of the most awesome jewelry from this lady down the street. No one's seen it but my mom and me. But—" Rebecca paused and glanced around, as if to make sure no one was listening. Then she wiggled her eyebrows at Alison. "—I could give you a special sneak preview, if you want."

Brenda frowned. "What about me? Don't I get a sneak preview, too?"

"But I thought you were going to buy the painting," Rebecca said innocently.

"I haven't decided for sure. Come on, let's see this jewelry." Brenda tossed her head and gestured for Rebecca to lead the way.

"Whew, that was close," Nancy said as Rebecca, Brenda, and Alison headed in the direction of the Ramirezes' garage. "If you're lucky, maybe Rebecca can talk Brenda into buying a necklace or something instead of the painting."

"Or maybe not," Bess said glumly. "I don't know, Nancy. I just *have* to figure out a way to get enough money to buy the painting before Brenda or anyone else."

"Oh, it's sublime! It's stunning! I *must* have it!"

Nancy and Bess turned around. It was the short, red-haired woman in the paint-spattered sundress. She was gazing intently at the ballerina painting and talking excitedly to no one in particular.

"You mean that?" Bess pointed to the painting.

"Yes. Look at the colors, the composition!" The woman began waving her hands. "They're inspired!"

"Are you an artist?" Bess asked the woman.

The woman nodded. "Luna Lamotte. I have a studio a couple of blocks away. My specialty is collages."

"We made collages at our school last week," Nancy said. "We cut up a bunch of pictures from magazines and glued them onto paper."

"That's like what I do. Except that I cut up other people's paintings, glue the pieces onto a canvas, and then kind of paint over them a little." Luna knelt down in front of the ballerina painting. "You see, this would be *perfect* for a new collage I'm working on."

Bess's jaw dropped. "Y-you want to cut this painting up into t-tiny little pieces?"

Just then a man walked up to the three of them. Nancy recognized him as one of the first early birds. He was the man in the suit and bow tie.

"Jamison Morris, at your service," he said. "I'm sure you all know who I am. I write the antiques column for the newspaper. The column is called 'Trash or Treasure?'" He turned to Luna. "Young

14

lady, I wouldn't waste my time on that painting if I were you."

Luna stood up. She looked confused. "Excuse me?"

"It's clearly the work of a Sunday painter—an amateur. The brushstrokes are inferior, and the colors are all wrong." Mr. Morris nodded in the direction of the garage. "Now, over there I saw a magnificent oil of the Greek goddess Athena. A far superior painting, in my opinion."

"Oh, I must have missed that one. I'll have to take a look." Luna smiled at Mr. Morris. "Thank you for the tip!" She headed toward the garage.

"Nancy! Bess!" Mrs. Ramirez yelled. She and George were moving some boxes from the front porch to the driveway. "Could you help us over here?"

"Sure, Mrs. Ramirez," Nancy yelled back.

On their way to the porch, Nancy and Bess passed Karen Koombs, who was checking out the lava lamp. Karen was in the fourth grade at Carl Sandburg Elementary.

"Hi, Karen," Nancy called out.

"Oh, hi." Karen pointed to the lava lamp. "I thought this might look cool in my room. My mom and dad are letting me redecorate it with a '60s theme."

"A '60s theme—that sounds awesome," Bess said.

Karen's gaze drifted past the two girls. "I saw you looking at that ballerina painting, Bess. Are you going to buy it or something?"

Bess made a face. "I really, really want to, but I have to raise the money first. And a bunch of other people are interested in it, too."

"That's too bad," Karen said.

Nancy and Bess said goodbye to Karen and joined Mrs. Ramirez and George on the porch. As Nancy began moving boxes, she glanced around the yard. More early birds had arrived, and the place was bustling.

Then Nancy noticed that Mr. Morris

was still standing at the gray card table where the ballerina painting was. He had picked the painting up and was looking at it very intently.

That's funny, Nancy thought. I thought he said he didn't like it.

"I could go home and ask for an advance on my allowance," Bess said to Nancy. "Except I already asked for an advance on my allowance last week, so my mom and dad would probably say no."

It was ten minutes till nine, and Bess and Nancy were doing some last-minute tasks for Mrs. Ramirez in the garage. Bess was still trying to figure out how she could get the ballerina painting before Brenda or Luna Lamotte or anyone else.

Looking around, Nancy was amazed at how tidy the Ramirezes' garage was. Usually, it was piled floor-to-ceiling with stuff and covered with dust and cobwebs, too. Now it was shiny and clean, with lots of merchandise organized neatly on card tables.

Nancy stuck a price tag on a pretty blue vase with pink polka dots on it. "I know," she said to Bess. "Why don't we ask Mrs. Ramirez if she can set the ballerina painting aside for you until your doll and your CD's sell?"

Bess sighed. "I already asked her that. She said that wouldn't be fair to the family that's selling the painting. I mean, if my stuff doesn't sell and I can't buy the painting, then the family might not get *their* money."

"That's true," Nancy said. She reached into her pocket. All she had was a dollar. "You have two dollars, and I have one. Even if I gave you this, we'd still need seven more—"

"Nancy! Bess!" George came running up to them. "Did you guys move it?"

"Move what? What are you talking about?" Nancy asked her.

"The ballerina painting," George replied breathlessly. "It's gone!"

3

A Mysterious Package

Gone! What are you talking about?" Bess cried out.

"It's gone," George replied. "It was over there, and now it's not."

Nancy, Bess, and George rushed over to the gray card table. George was right. The painting was no longer there.

"Maybe someone moved it," Nancy suggested.

"Come on, let's look around," Bess said.

The three girls spent the next few minutes combing the yard. They looked on top of tables and under tables. They looked inside boxes. They looked behind other paintings. But the ballerina was nowhere to be found.

The Ramirezes' yard was really crowded with customers now.

Nancy peeked at someone's watch. It was two minutes before nine o'clock, just about time for the garage sale to start.

Mrs. Ramirez came by just then. She had her clipboard in one hand and a metal cash box in the other. "Girls, we need to take our places," she said, sounding a little flustered. "Bess and George, I need you over on the porch to take cash from our customers and make out receipts. Nancy, why don't you and Rebecca roam around and answer any questions people might have."

"Okay," Nancy said. "Oh, Mrs. Ramirez? Did you move that ballerina painting Bess wanted to buy?"

Mrs. Ramirez frowned. "Move it? No, of course not." A woman passed by just then, and Mrs. Ramirez rushed toward her. "Ellie! Oh, Ellie! I wanted to talk to you about that box of encyclopedias you dropped off."

Bess turned to Nancy, looking troubled. "If Mrs. Ramirez didn't move the painting, then what could have happened to it?"

"Maybe someone stole it," George suggested.

"Stole it!" Bess exclaimed.

"We'd better get to work," Nancy said quickly. "Rebecca and I will keep looking for the painting while we're walking around, okay?"

"Okay, I guess," Bess said with a heavy sigh. "I hope you guys find it. I really love that painting."

Nancy found Rebecca arranging a bunch of old books on a card table. She told her about the missing painting.

"Your mom wants us to walk around and answer questions and stuff," Nancy finished. "I thought we could look for the painting while we were doing that."

"Let's split up," Rebecca suggested.

"Isn't that what detectives do when they, um, detect?"

Nancy giggled. "Yeah, I guess. Why don't you take the driveway and garage, and I'll take the front yard?"

Nancy took her time walking around the Ramirezes' yard. She went through all the cardboard boxes that she, Bess, and George had missed the first time around. She looked underneath a pile of pretty antique quilts. She rooted through a bunch of old velvet and lace dresses that were hanging up. She checked out all the customers, to see if any of them was carrying the painting. But no one was.

"Hey, Nancy!"

Nancy turned around. Brenda was standing there. She was holding a couple of CD's in one hand and a butterfly-shaped rhinestone pin in the other.

"Hi, Brenda," Nancy said. "You found some stuff to buy, huh?"

Brenda tossed her brown hair over her shoulders. "Yeah, I guess. I was going to buy that ballerina painting, but I can't find it anywhere. Did someone else already buy it?"

"Actually, it's kind of missing," Nancy admitted.

"Missing!" Brenda let out a mean-sounding laugh. "Boy, you guys aren't very good at your jobs, are you? You can't even keep track of the merchandise."

"So you haven't seen it?" Nancy asked her.

Brenda gave Nancy a funny look. "Seen it? What are you talking about? I haven't seen it since Alison and I were looking at it with all of you."

Brenda said goodbye and headed for the front porch. There, Mrs. Ramirez, Bess, and George were busy taking money from people. Nancy was about to dig through another cardboard box when she felt a hand on her elbow.

"Excuse me. You haven't seen the ballerina painting, have you?"

It was the artist Luna Lamotte. She was holding a different painting in her

arms: the painting of the Greek goddess Athena.

"I'm going to use this in my collage," Luna explained, nodding at the painting. "But I also decided that I wanted to use that ballerina painting, too. I'm going to call the piece 'Women, Girls, and Goddesses.'" She smiled at Nancy. "So do you know where it is? The ballerina painting, I mean?"

"Um, we sort of can't find it," Nancy replied.

Luna raised her eyebrows. "You can't find it? Whatever do you mean?"

"I mean, we can't find it," Nancy repeated. "It's been lost . . . or stolen."

Luna looked upset. "Oh, I hope not. It's a very nice painting." She added, "If it turns up, will you let me know?"

"No problem," Nancy said.

After Luna Lamotte left, Nancy poured herself a cup of cranberry juice at the refreshment table and took a big gulp. Her thoughts were racing. What could have happened to the ballerina painting?

Could someone really have stolen it? But who?

As Nancy finished up her juice, she noticed a girl from her school checking out her blue parka. It looked as if the girl might buy it. Nancy was glad. That meant that she would have enough money to buy the gold pen with the *N* on it.

Then she saw Mr. Morris standing by one of the card tables, inspecting an old silver pocket watch. He was also talking to a woman. Nancy recognized her as one of the Ramirezes' neighbors.

"Garage-sale items that might seem worthless to most people may actually be very valuable," Mr. Morris was saying to the woman. "For example, there was a rhinestone pin someone bought at a Pennsylvania garage sale for two dollars. It turned out to be made of real diamonds. And there was a painting someone bought in California for twenty dollars. It ended up selling for a million dollars at a New York City auction."

"A million dollars!" the woman

exclaimed. "My, that's a lot of money! I guess I should take a look around and see if I might be able to find something valuable, too."

"It takes a good eye and a great deal of patience," Mr. Morris stated. "I wrote about that in my column, 'Trash or Treasure?' last week. Of course you read my column, don't you?"

As Nancy listened to Mr. Morris talk, she had a thought. He was the last person she had seen with the ballerina painting. He might know something about where it was.

But just then Nancy was distracted by a strange sight.

Brenda was heading down the sidewalk, away from the Ramirezes' house. She was carrying something in her arms—something wrapped in a black garbage bag. It was big and flat.

Maybe it's the ballerina painting! Nancy said to herself.

4

The Plot Thickens

Nancy started running in Brenda's direction, but Brenda had had a big head start. She was almost to the corner already.

"Brenda!" Nancy yelled, waving her arms. But Brenda didn't seem to notice her. "Hey, Brenda—*oof!*"

Nancy's foot caught on something, and she went flying to the ground. She landed in a heap on the grass.

"What was that?" she said out loud. She rubbed her elbows, then rose to her feet.

Nancy turned around to see what she had tripped over. Behind her on the grass was an upside-down cardboard box. CD's had spilled everywhere.

"Oh, great," she muttered. She glanced in Brenda's direction, but Brenda was gone.

Nancy thought about trying to find her but changed her mind. She had to put the CD's back in the cardboard box.

Five minutes later Nancy walked up to the front porch, where Bess, George, and Mrs. Ramirez were collecting money. Bess held up half a blueberry muffin. "You want part of this, Nancy?" she said between bites.

"No, thanks," Nancy said. "I have a question. Did any of you just sell something to Brenda?"

"Brenda Carlton? I don't think so," Mrs. Ramirez replied.

"Something big and flat?" Nancy asked.

"No. But let me double check." Mrs. Ramirez flipped through the copies of the receipts. "I was right. There are no receipts here made out to Brenda."

A bunch of customers appeared just then, wanting to pay for their merchandise. Bess, George, and Mrs. Ramirez got busy helping them out. Nancy wandered away, her thoughts racing like mad. If Brenda didn't buy anything, then it was even more likely that the package had contained the ballerina painting.

Could Brenda really be a thief? Nancy wondered. Had she wanted the ballerina painting *that* badly?

"Wow, we made a fortune!" Rebecca exclaimed. She waved a wad of bills in the air. "Three hundred and ten dollars!"

It was five o'clock, and the last of the customers had just left. Rebecca and Mrs. Ramirez were adding up the money in the cash box. Then they checked the amount against the paper receipts. Nancy, Bess, and George were packing up some stuff nearby.

The sun was still shining brightly, even though it was late in the day. As Nancy worked, she glanced around the

Ramirezes' yard. It looked really pretty, with all the daffodils, tulips, and other spring flowers. She wiped a bead of sweat off her forehead. She was hot and tired, but it was a nice kind of hot and tired because she'd had fun working at the sale.

Mrs. Ramirez punched some numbers into a calculator. "That's strange," she said, frowning. "We have three hundred and ten dollars in cash, right? But I count only three hundred dollars' worth of receipts."

"No way." Rebecca counted the cash again. After a moment, she said, "Yup, it's definitely three hundred and ten dollars."

"Maybe one of us forgot to make out a receipt or two," Mrs. Ramirez said thoughtfully. "It's not a big deal, really, except that we need to make sure we give all the sellers the money they're due."

Ten dollars, Nancy thought, listening to Mrs. Ramirez. Now, why did that number ring a bell?

* * *

"So you think Brenda stole my balle-rina painting?" Bess asked Nancy.

Bess, Nancy, and George were walking over to Brenda's house on their way home from the Ramirezes'. Nancy had told George and Bess about the big, flat package she'd seen Brenda carrying. Nancy really wanted to ask Brenda about it.

"I don't know," Nancy said in answer to Bess's question. "Maybe. Brenda did say she might want to buy the painting for her room. What if she decided, you know, to beat out the competition by just kind of stealing it?"

"What competition?" George piped up.

"Well, there's Bess," Nancy replied. "And Luna Lamotte said she wanted the painting, too. And there could have been other people."

They soon reached Brenda's house. Nancy went up to the door and knocked. There was no answer.

"Try the doorbell," George suggested.

Nancy rang the doorbell: once, twice, three times. There was still no answer.

"I guess no one's home," Nancy said with a sigh.

"Too bad we can't just go in and look for the painting ourselves," Bess said.

"Ten dollars!" Nancy said suddenly. "That's the price of the ballerina painting!"

Bess rolled her eyes. "Of course it's the price of the ballerina painting. I've only been talking about it all day long."

Nancy shook her head. "No, I mean, what Mrs. Ramirez was saying. Okay, listen to this. What if Brenda or somebody took the ballerina painting without letting anybody know? But then the person slipped ten dollars into the cash box when you guys weren't looking?"

George nodded. "I get it. That way, it wouldn't seem like it was really stealing."

Bess slapped herself on the side of the head. "I just thought of something, too. I was going to tell you guys earlier, but I totally forgot about it."

"What?" Nancy asked her curiously.

"That man, Mr. Moore . . . Morrison . . ." Bess began.

"Morris," Nancy said.

Bess nodded. "Right, Morris. Anyway, remember how he told Luna Lamotte that the ballerina painting was no good? Well, after she left, I saw him looking at the painting. I mean, *really* looking at it."

"I saw him doing that, too," Nancy said.

"Did you see him looking at it with that bizarre magnifying glass, though?" Bess asked her. "He was going over the whole painting with it as if he wanted to buy it. Which is weird, because of what he told Ms. Lamotte."

Nancy fell silent. She thought about Mr. Morris's strange behavior. Had he been hiding something? Nancy wondered. Was *he* the thief and not Brenda?

5

The List of Suspects

P ass the cheese, please!" Nancy said. "And the guacamole. Oh, and the sour cream, too."

It was make-your-own-tacos night at Nancy's house. Hannah Gruen, the Drews' housekeeper, had taco night at least once a month. Hannah had taken care of Nancy ever since her mother had died five years earlier.

Nancy's father, Carson Drew, picked up the bowls of grated cheese, guacamole, and sour cream and passed them across the table to Nancy. Nancy had already heaped a bunch of chicken, lettuce, and tomato chunks into a crunchy taco shell. Now she added the other ingredients.

"That's your third taco, Pudding Pie," Mr. Drew said with a smile. "You must be awfully hungry."

"Working at the garage sale all day must have given you an appetite," Hannah said.

Nancy bit into her taco, which was stuffed and really gooey. It was delicious. "Yup. Plus, I have a new mystery to solve, too."

Mr. Drew chuckled. "I should have known. It seems as if you can't go anywhere without running into a mystery. You're a regular mystery magnet, Pudding Pie."

"So tell us—what's the mystery?" Hannah prompted her.

Nancy put down her taco and wiped her mouth with a napkin. Then she told her dad and Hannah the story of the missing ballerina painting.

When she finished, Mr. Drew steepled

his hands under his chin and said, "Hmm, sounds like an interesting case. Do you have any suspects so far?"

Nancy nodded. "Brenda's my main suspect. She wanted to buy the painting. Plus, I saw her carrying that package from the Ramirezes' house."

"The package could have been something else," Hannah pointed out.

Nancy shrugged. "I guess. But it was flat like the painting and kind of the same size, too." She added, "My other suspect is Mr. Morris."

"I love that column of his, 'Trash or Treasure?'" Hannah said enthusiastically. "I have an old map of this area that used to belong to my grandfather. I didn't think it was worth much, but then Mr. Morris did a column on maps a few months ago. According to him, maps like mine can be worth a couple of hundred dollars, maybe even more."

"Why do you suspect Jamison Morris, Nancy?" Mr. Drew asked her. "He's a fairly respected man around these

parts—you know, being a journalist and an antiques expert and all."

Nancy took another bite of her taco and chewed thoughtfully. "Mr. Morris told Luna Lamotte that the painting was worthless," she said finally. "But then I saw him looking at it again. And Bess told me later that she saw him looking at it a *lot*, with some sort of special magnifying glass."

"So let me get this straight. You think he wanted the painting for himself. But he told Luna Lamotte that it was worthless so she'd lose interest in it?" Mr. Drew said slowly.

Nancy nodded. "Uh-huh. I heard him talking to this lady about how stuff at garage sales can sometimes turn out to be worth lots of money. He even mentioned some painting that someone bought for twenty dollars. It turned out to be worth a million dollars!"

She added, "What if Mr. Morris thought that the ballerina painting was worth lots and lots of money? Maybe he decided to steal it before anyone else could buy it."

"Interesting theory," Mr. Drew remarked. "Any other suspects? You mentioned that Luna Lamotte wanted the painting, too, right?"

"Right. Hmm. I guess I should add her to the suspect list, too," Nancy said, nodding.

Hannah got up from the table and started to clear the dishes. "Dessert, anyone? I made a strawberry pie, and I think we have some vanilla ice cream in the freezer." She grinned. "Or are we all too full of tacos?"

"We're never too full for your strawberry pie—are we?" Mr. Drew said, winking at his daughter.

Nancy winked back. "No way."

Later that night Nancy put on her favorite pink nightgown, brushed her teeth, and washed her face. Then she went to say good night to her father and Hannah.

Mr. Drew was in his study going over some work. "Have you solved the mystery yet?" he asked Nancy, his eyes twinkling.

She kissed him on the cheek. "Not yet, Daddy. But I'm working on it."

After saying good night to Hannah, Nancy went to her room. She got her special blue notebook out of her desk. The notebook helped her to organize her thoughts whenever she was trying to solve a mystery.

She got into bed and snuggled under the covers. She opened the notebook to a blank page and thought for a moment. Then she began to write.

"The Case of the Missing Painting," she scribbled. Under that, she wrote: "Suspects." She skipped a line and added: "Brenda Carlton: Wanted the painting for her room. Was carrying a garbage bag with something big and flat in it. Mr. Morris: Bess saw him looking at the painting with a magnifying glass. Might think the painting is worth a lot of money. Luna Lamotte: Wanted the painting for her collage."

Nancy stopped writing and glanced around her room. She thought about how Bess wanted the ballerina painting for *her* room, and Brenda, too. She thought about Karen Koombs, who had also been at the garage sale that morning. Karen had mentioned that she was totally redecorating her room with a '60s theme.

Nancy liked her room just as it was — she couldn't imagine selling any of her furniture, or buying anything new either.

"But I guess I might change my mind someday," she told herself. She imagined all the different themes she could choose for her room: a unicorn theme, a flower theme, a wild animal theme.

"Or maybe even a mystery theme," she said, giggling.

She turned her attention back to her blue notebook and read over her new entry several times. She felt as though she was missing some important piece of the puzzle — something obvious. But she couldn't put her finger on it.

Her eyelids were starting to droop a

little. It was late, and she had to be at the Ramirezes' bright and early for the second day of the garage sale.

"Maybe I'll be able to figure it all out tomorrow," she murmured sleepily to herself. Then she closed the blue notebook, put it on her nightstand, and turned out the light.

"It looks like it's going to rain," George remarked.

It was Sunday morning. Nancy, Bess, and George were walking over to the Ramirezes' house. While Saturday had been bright and warm and sunny, this day was different. The sky was gray and full of clouds, and the air felt thick and damp.

"I talked to my parents, and they said they'd give me five dollars toward next week's allowance," Bess told her friends. "I have two dollars, so I just need three more to buy the ballerina painting. There's just one problem . . ."

"The painting's gone." Nancy stuffed

her hands into the pockets of her jeans. "Maybe we should talk to all our suspects again: Mr. Morris, Luna Lamotte, and Brenda. Especially Brenda."

"Why don't we try her house again?" George suggested. "Maybe she'll be home this time."

"Good idea," Nancy agreed.

The three girls turned the corner and crossed the street. They soon reached Brenda's house.

They started to walk up to the Carltons' front door. But something caught Nancy's attention.

"Look!" she exclaimed, pointing.

Brenda was hurrying across her backyard. And she was carrying the big, flat package from the day before!

6

A Scary Noise

Nancy went running up to Brenda. George and Bess followed. "Brenda! Hey, Brenda!" Nancy called out.

Brenda stopped in her tracks. She glared at Nancy and her friends. "What are you guys doing here?" she asked suspiciously.

"We want to know what's in that package," George said.

"This?" Brenda set the package down on the grass and stared at the three girls. "None of your business!"

"It's the ballerina painting, isn't it?"

Bess blurted out. "You stole it from the garage sale!"

"What?" Brenda looked as if she didn't believe what she was hearing. Then she burst out laughing. "You're kidding, right?"

Nancy, George, and Bess exchanged glances. "Uh, no, not really," Bess said. "Nancy saw you taking that package from the garage sale yesterday."

"You're crazy!" Brenda cried out. "This is *not* the ballerina painting."

"What is it, then?" George asked her.

Brenda hesitated. "Not that I have to explain it to the three of you," she said finally. "But it's an antique frame. The lady who lives next door, Mrs. Mannheim, bought it at the garage sale. She's kind of old and frail and she couldn't carry it home, so she asked me to do it."

"But that was yesterday, right?" Nancy pointed out. "Why do you still have it?"

Brenda rolled her eyes. "When I was walking home with it yesterday, I acci-

dentally dropped it on the sidewalk. A piece of it chipped off. So my mom and I fixed it with a special kind of glue that had to dry overnight. Now I'm taking it over to Mrs. Mannheim's house." She made a face at Nancy. "Are you satisfied now? Can I go?"

Bess sighed. "Oh, well. I guess that means the painting's still missing."

"Why do you care so much about that stupid old painting?" Brenda asked her.

"Stupid!" Bess said, her blue eyes widening. "I thought you liked that painting!"

"I did. But I changed my mind. It really wasn't *that* great." Brenda tossed her hair over shoulders. "Why is everyone making such a big deal about it, anyway?"

"I just felt a drop," Mrs. Ramirez said, lifting her face to the sky.

It was nine o'clock, time for the garage sale to start. But there were only a couple

50

of customers waiting in the driveway. Nancy figured that the weather must be keeping people away. The sky was full of dark clouds now, and it was starting to rain a little.

There were still a lot of items around—items that hadn't sold the day before. Nancy, Bess, George, and Rebecca had just finished helping Mrs. Ramirez arrange these things on card tables. Nancy noticed that George's toy kitchen, Bess's CD's and doll, and Rebecca's old Halloween costumes were among them. Her own blue parka and George's baseball glove were not. They had been snapped up early yesterday morning.

Nancy also noticed that the gold pen with the initial *N* was still available. So were the comic books and board game George wanted, and Rebecca's pink necklace.

Mrs. Ramirez looked around now and frowned.

"We'd better cover everything up

before the rain really gets going," she said. "There are some plastic tarps in the garage. Come on, girls."

Mrs. Ramirez headed toward the garage. Rebecca, Bess, and George followed. Nancy was about to follow, too, when she felt a tap on her shoulder.

She stopped and turned around. It was Luna Lamotte. She was wearing a white T-shirt and jeans that were covered with red and purple paint.

"Hello! It's me again," Luna said with a smile. "I was wondering. Did that ballerina painting ever turn up?"

"No," Nancy replied. "We're still looking, though."

Luna shook her head "That's such a shame. The more I thought about it, the more I realized that it would be perfect for my women, girls, and goddesses collage. And I'm opening a show of my work in just a few weeks. Oh, yes, speaking of which . . ."

Luna reached into her jeans pocket and pulled out a folded-up pink postcard. It had a picture of a brightly colored collage on it. "Here's an invitation to the opening. Maybe you and your friends could come—and your parents, too. It'll be in my studio, which is just a couple of blocks away."

"Thanks a lot," Nancy said, taking the postcard. She turned it over in her hand. It said: "Luna Lamotte: Recent Works. Opening Reception April 22, 2-4 P.M. 245 Montague Street. Everyone welcome!"

After Luna left, Nancy helped Mrs. Ramirez and the others put plastic tarps over all the tables. While they were working, she saw a familiar figure coming up the driveway. It was Jamison Morris.

"What? You're not closing shop, are you?" he snapped at Nancy.

"We're just covering everything up because of the rain," Nancy explained. She wondered why Mr. Morris had returned.

As if reading her mind, Mr. Morris said, "There was a silver pocket watch here yesterday. I wasn't going to buy it, but then I had a change of heart. Is it still available, young lady?"

"Hmm. I think someone bought that," Nancy replied.

Mr. Morris frowned. "I *knew* I should have grabbed it when I had the chance. He who hesitates, et cetera." He turned to go.

"Excuse me, Mr. Morris?" Nancy said. "Do you remember that painting of the ballerina?"

Mr. Morris raised his eyebrows. "What? Oh, yes, that worthless old thing. What of it?"

"Worthless? But you were looking at it a lot," Nancy pointed out.

"I was looking at it because I was trying to see if there was a signature. I was curious about whether the artist was a local person." Mr. Morris stared at Nancy with a strange expression. "Why do you ask, young lady?"

"Well, it's missing," Nancy replied. "I'm just trying to figure out if anyone might know anything about it."

"Missing, is it? Well, it's no great loss, I assure you." Mr. Morris paused. "You're not suggesting that I know anything about it, are you?"

"Well, no, but—" Nancy began.

Mr. Morris narrowed his eyes at her. "I would be careful about accusing people of such things if I were you, young lady. Especially someone like me. I'm a very important man." And with that, he turned on his heels and left.

"He was pretty mad at me," Nancy told George, Bess, and Rebecca.

It was ten A.M. The four of them were walking over to Montague Street, to Luna Lamotte's studio. Because the rain seemed to be keeping the customers away, Mrs. Ramirez had told them that they could take a little break. Nancy had gotten the idea to check out Luna Lamotte's studio, to see if the ballerina painting might be there.

Bess huddled closer to Nancy. The two of them were sharing a yellow umbrella

55

that they'd borrowed from the Ramirezes. George and Rebecca were sharing an orange one.

"Do you think Mr. Morris took my painting?" Bess asked Nancy.

Nancy shrugged. "I'm not sure. I think we need more evidence."

Nancy pulled the pink postcard out of her jeans pocket and glanced at the address. "Number 245 Montague Street—there it is." She pointed to a big purple house with blue shutters. In the back was a large purple barn with big windows and skylights.

"I bet that barn is Ms. Lamotte's studio," George said.

"Wow, *I'd* like a cool studio like that," Rebecca said, her eyes shining. "I could store all my costumes there, and we could put on plays and stuff. *The Case of the Missing Painting*, starring Rebecca Ramirez. *The Garage Sale Mystery*, starring Rebecca Ramirez."

Nancy giggled, then crossed the yard in

the direction of the studio. The other girls followed.

When they got closer to the studio, they stopped in their tracks. "Listen!" Bess whispered.

Nancy's heart began beating faster. A really scary noise was coming from inside the studio. It sounded like someone screaming!

7

A Sticky Clue

Nancy listened carefully. She heard the noise again. It was a really strange noise, not quite human. It sounded like the cries of an animal or the screeching of an out-of-tune violin.

Nancy tried to ignore the wild beating of her heart. There's nothing to be afraid of, she told herself. But she didn't quite believe it.

She tiptoed up to one of the oversize windows and peered inside. The pane was grimy and paint-covered, and it was a little hard to see through it.

Luna Lamotte's studio was one big room with really high ceilings. There were tall shelves filled with vases of dried flowers, seashells, potted plants, and antique dolls. The floor was covered with paint-spattered dropcloths. There were buckets of brushes and cans of paint of all different colors: red, blue, yellow, green, black, white, purple, silver, gold.

Luna Lamotte was standing in the far corner of the room. She was dressed in a really weird outfit: a long white robe and big goggles.

"Where's that noise coming from?" George whispered over Nancy's shoulder.

"This is too creepy," Bess complained. "Let's get out of here!"

"Wait!" Nancy pressed her face closer to the pane. "Look, guys! I think she's sawing something."

The four of them squinted to see through the grimy window. Nancy was right. Luna Lamotte was running a saw back and forth across a canvas. The motion of the saw was making the strange, screechy sound.

"It's my ballerina!" Bess cried out. "She's cutting it up!"

Nancy frowned. "Wasn't the ballerina painting mostly white and pink and purple?"

Bess hesitated. "Uh, yeah. Why?"

Nancy nodded at the canvas Luna Lamotte was sawing. "That looks like it's mostly yellow and red."

Bess stared. "Huh. You're right."

"I don't see any paintings in there that look like the ballerina painting," George said, glancing around. "There's that Athena painting over there in the corner, and another one next to it with a bunch of fish on it. But no ballerina."

"Maybe Ms. Lamotte's innocent after all," Nancy said thoughtfully.

"Hmm. Now what?" Rebecca said with a sigh. "We're totally out of suspects."

"Now I think we need something to inspire us," Bess said.

* * *

"Mmm. Double Trouble Caramel-Fudge Fantasy," Rebecca said, licking her ice cream cone. "My favorite!"

"Mine is better. Super-Duper Strawberry Bananarama," Bess said, licking her cone. "It's got marshmallow bits in it, too. Yum!"

After leaving Luna Lamotte's studio, Bess and the others had gone over to the Marvins' house. Bess had convinced her mother to take them to the Double Dip for ice cream cones. Now the four girls were munching on their cones and walking from the Marvins' house to the Ramirezes'. The rain had stopped, and the sun was peeking out from behind the clouds.

Nancy took off her jeans jacket and wrapped it around her waist. She took a bite of her cone. The ice cream was a flavor she'd never had before, called Peppermint Partytime. It was pink, full of peppermint candies—and super-yummy.

Still, she couldn't totally enjoy it. She had a mystery to solve, and she had reached a dead end, kind of. None of her suspects seemed to know anything about the missing painting.

Nancy took another bite of her cone. Just then an idea came to her. She stopped in her tracks.

George, who was walking behind her, slammed into her. "Hey, Nancy! I almost got my Very Scary Blueberry all over you!" she exclaimed.

"Oh, sorry, George," Nancy said. Her blue eyes were sparkling. "Listen, everyone. I just had an idea. Who owns the ballerina painting?"

"What?" Bess said. "No one does. It's missing, remember?"

Nancy shook her head. "No, I mean— who put it in the garage sale?"

"Oh." Rebecca took a bite of her ice cream cone. "I don't remember. Let's go to my house and ask my mom to check the list."

"Why do you care who owns the painting?" George asked Nancy curiously.

"I'm not sure. I just have this feeling

that it could be an important clue," Nancy replied.

The girls walked and finished up their ice cream cones in silence. Just before they got to Rebecca's house, they ran into Karen Koombs, who was walking in the opposite direction.

"Hey, Karen!" Nancy called out. She popped the last bite of her cone into her mouth. "Were you just at the garage sale?"

Karen stopped and stuffed her hands into the pockets of her jeans jacket. "Uh, yeah. Are you guys going there now?"

"Yeah. Remember that ballerina painting?" Bess spoke up. "Somebody stole it! We've been looking for it since yesterday, and we even have a bunch of suspects. So if you see or hear anything suspicious . . ."

Karen's gaze dropped to the ground. Nancy noticed that she suddenly seemed awfully uncomfortable.

Then Nancy noticed another thing.

Something small and white was stuck to the sleeve of Karen's jeans jacket. It was a sticker, and it said: "#23/$10."

Nancy stared at Karen. "*You* took the ballerina painting, didn't you?" she said slowly.

8

Case Closed!

Karen's face turned bright red. "Yes," she said in a voice barely above a whisper.

Bess, George, and Rebecca gaped at her, and then at Nancy. "How did you know?" Bess asked Nancy.

Nancy pointed to the sticker on Karen's sleeve. "That's the price tag from the ballerina painting," Nancy explained. "I watched your mom make it up, Rebecca. The number twenty-three is the seller, and—"

"*I'm* the seller," Karen blurted out. "It's my painting."

"What!" Nancy, Bess, George, and Rebecca exclaimed together.

"I didn't guess *that* part!" Nancy added.

Karen folded her arms across her chest. "See, I'd been bugging my mom and dad for a long time about redecorating my room. They finally said yes. But they said I'd have to sell my old stuff first, to make room for the new stuff."

"So you decided to sell the ballerina painting," George prompted her.

"Right," Karen replied. "The ballerina painting, plus some furniture and a bunch of other things, too."

Rebecca shook her head. She looked really confused. "I don't get it. Why would you steal your own painting? I mean, that's totally weird."

"I know." Karen took a deep breath. "See, I've had that painting for a really long time," she went on. "I guess I liked it more than I thought. But I was kind of embarrassed about changing my mind about selling it. So . . . well . . . I, um. . . ."

"You kind of took it out of the garage sale without telling anyone," Nancy finished for her.

Karen nodded. "Exactly."

"I can understand that," Bess told Karen. "I put some old CD's and this doll I used to play with in the garage sale. But then I started thinking about my doll and how much fun I used to have with her. I almost took her out of the sale."

Karen smiled a little. "So why didn't you?"

Bess shrugged. "I really, really wanted the ballerina painting. And I needed to raise the money to buy it. So I figured it was worth selling my doll if I could get the painting."

"Wow," Karen said. "I didn't realize you wanted my painting so much."

"Why don't we all go to Rebecca's house together and explain what happened to her mom?" Nancy suggested.

"I'm sorry I caused all this trouble," Karen apologized.

Nancy grinned. "Don't worry about it, Karen. It's always fun having a mystery to solve!"

That afternoon the garage sale was a mob scene. The sun was shining, and lots of people were out enjoying the day. Nancy, Bess, George, and Rebecca were busy helping Mrs. Ramirez take care of customers. Karen had offered to help, too, and was assisting with the receipts.

By the end of the day, almost all the merchandise was gone. George's toy kitchen, Rebecca's Halloween costumes, and Bess's doll and old CD's had all sold. With the money, George was able to buy the board game she'd wanted, and Rebecca got her pink necklace. Nancy was able to buy the gold pen with the initial *N* on it.

Bess came up to Nancy, Karen, and Mrs. Ramirez, who were adding up receipts on the porch. "Well, I've got my ten dollars now," she said, holding up a stack of one-dollar bills. "I don't have anything to buy, though," she added in a glum voice.

Karen and Mrs. Ramirez exchanged a glance. "Well, actually, there's this cool ballerina painting you might be interested in," Karen said with a smile.

Bess's eyes got as big as saucers. "What? I thought you decided not to sell it."

"I know. But I changed my mind—again. I really do want a whole new look for my room." Karen added, "Plus, I can tell that you really love that painting. So you should have it."

"Karen and I discussed it," Mrs. Ramirez spoke up. "I called Brenda Carlton, Luna Lamotte, and Jamison Morris on the phone, to make sure it was okay with them that Karen sells you the painting. They all said yes—even Mr. Morris."

Bess grinned. "Yes! This is so awesome! I can't wait to hang the painting in my room!" She turned to Karen. "Thank you, thank you, thank you."

"You're welcome," Karen said, giggling. "Just take good care of it, okay?"

Mrs. Ramirez held up a stack of receipts. "Oh, by the way, Nancy—I thought you'd be interested. Remember that extra ten dollars I couldn't account for yesterday?"

Nancy nodded. "Did you ever figure that out?"

"I made a mistake," Mrs. Ramirez admitted. "I must have hit the wrong button on my calculator or something. Anyway, we're all squared away with the numbers—we made six hundred dollars in two days."

Mrs. Ramirez added, "Thanks to you girls. You were a big help!"

"Any time," Bess said. "Now, who wants to come to my house to help me hang up my new painting?"

Half an hour later, Nancy, George, Bess, Rebecca, and Karen found themselves in Bess's bedroom. Bess and Karen were standing on top of the bed,

holding the ballerina painting against the wall.

"More to the left," George was saying.

"No, more to the right," Rebecca corrected her.

They finally got the painting centered on the wall just right. Bess hammered in a nail and hung up the picture. Then she hopped off her bed and stared at it with a big smile on her face.

"It's perfect," she said with a sigh.

"It does look really great in here," Karen agreed. "Take good care of it, okay?"

"You can visit it anytime you miss it," Bess told her.

While the girls were chatting, Nancy sat down in a big stuffed chair in a corner of the room. She pulled her blue notebook out of the pocket of her jeans jacket, and also her new pen that she'd bought at the garage sale. She stared at the pen for a moment, at the pretty gold color and the way the initial *N* curved so elegantly. Then she began to write.

* * *

Sometimes it can be hard to let go of things you think you've outgrown. But letting go of old stuff means you make room for new stuff. And getting new stuff is fun—almost as fun as solving a mystery!

Case closed.

EASY TO READ—FUN TO SOLVE!

**Meet up with suspense and mystery
in The Hardy Boys® are:**

THE CLUES™
BROTHERS

Available from Minstrel® Books
Published by Pocket Books

2389